This book belongs to

....

....

A catalogue record for this book is available from the British Library
Published by Ladybird Books Ltd.
A Penguin Company
80 Strand, London, WC2R 0RL, England
Penguin Books Australia Ltd, 250 Camberwell Road,
Camberwell, Victoria 3124, Australia
New York, Canada, India, New Zealand, South Africa

001 - 10 9 8 7 6 5 4 3 2 1

© Eric Hill, 2004
This edition published 2011
Eric Hill has asserted his moral rights under the
Copyright, Designs and Patents Act of 1988
All rights reserved
Planned and produced by Ventura Publishing Ltd
80 Strand, London WC2R 0RL

ISBN 978-0-72326-757-7

Printed in China

Spot's
New Game

Eric Hill

Spot and Tom were in the garden.
"When you've finished on the
swing, can we play a game?"
asked Tom.
"OK," said Spot. "Let's play
hide-and-seek."
"That's not much fun with just
the two of us," said Tom.

Just then, Helen and Steve looked over the fence.

"Yoo-hoo, Spot!" said Helen.
"Can we play with you and Tom?"
"Yes!" said Spot. "We can play
hide-and-seek. You can hide and
I'll shut my eyes and count
to ten. Then watch out!"

Spot started to count. Helen, Tom
and Steve ran around finding
places to hide.
"One, two, three..." said Spot.

"Where shall I hide?" said Helen.

Tom and Steve had disappeared and Spot was still counting. "Four, five, six..." said Spot.

Then, Helen found a hiding place.

"Seven, eight, nine...ten!" Spot opened his eyes. "Here I come!"

Spot looked around. There was no sign of Helen, or Tom, or Steve.

Spot looked behind the fence.
"Nobody there," said the
blue bird, as it flew away.

Spot walked past a rose bush.
"Mmm, that's a nice smell,"
said Spot.

Then Spot stopped. He heard a
noise coming from behind the bush.
It was a giggle – definitely
a giggle!

"I've never heard a bush giggle,"
said Spot, and he looked behind
the bush.

"Found you, Helen!" said Spot.
"I heard you giggle."
"Oops!" said Helen. "I was
enjoying myself too much!"

Spot carried on looking for
the others, but there was no sign
of Tom or Steve. Spot even looked
inside the wheelbarrow.

"You woke me up!" said Ginger
cat. "I was having a nice dream."
"Sorry!" said Spot.

Spot went a bit further down the garden path and stopped by a tree. He heard another giggle.

"I haven't heard a tree giggle, either," said Spot.

He looked up and shouted, "Come down, Steve! I heard you giggle."

Steve jumped down from
the tree.
"Have you found Tom yet?"
he asked.
"Not yet," said Spot.

Suddenly, a loud noise came
from the shed and a rabbit
jumped out from behind a
flowerpot. Then Spot heard
another giggle.

Spot opened the shed door and there was Tom.

"What was that noise?"
asked Spot.
"Oh, I was giggling so much
I knocked down a flowerpot," said
Tom. "I like this game...
if only I could stop giggling!"

27

"Well," said Spot, "now that
I've found everyone, I think
we should play the game again.
That was fun."

Helen smiled.
"Yes, but this time we can call the
game hide-and-giggle!"

And that started off another
round of giggles.

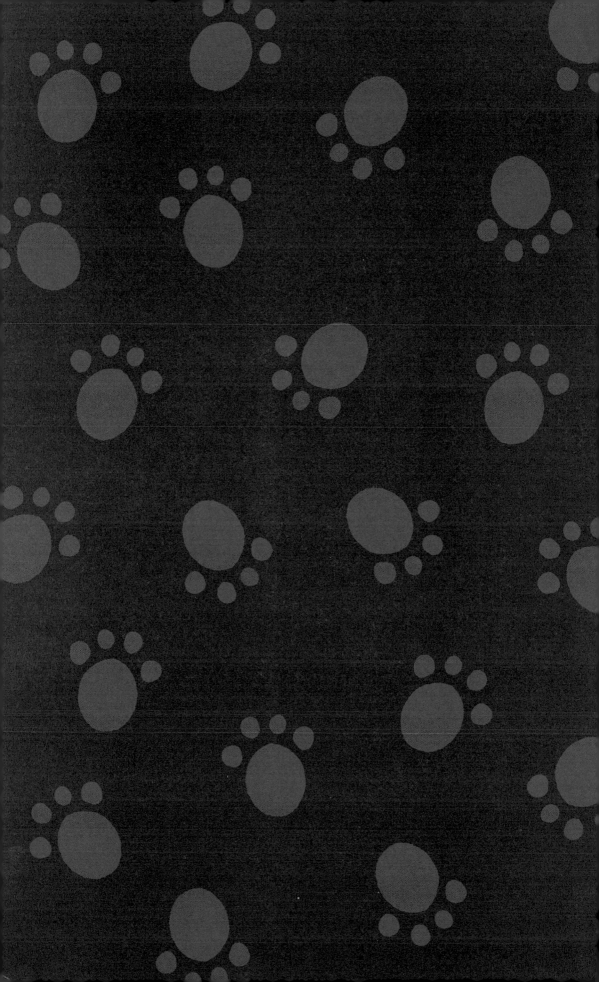

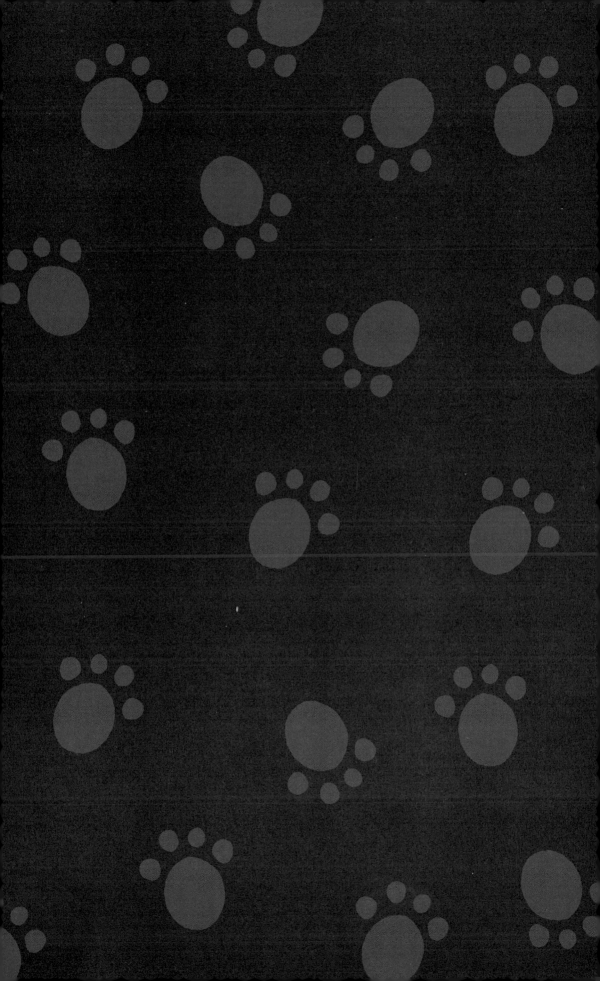